The Red Fox

Peter Leigh

Hodder Murray

A MEMBER OF THE HODDER HEADLINE GROUP

Hodder Headline's policy is to use papers that are natural, renewable and recyclable products and made from wood grown in sustainable forests. The logging and manufacturing processes are expected to conform to the environmental regulations of the country of origin.

Orders: please contact Bookpoint Ltd, 130 Milton Park, Abingdon, Oxon OX14 4SB. Telephone: (44) 01235 827720. Fax: (44) 01235 400454. Lines are open from 9.00am to 5.00pm, Monday to Saturday, with a 24-hour message answering service.
Visit our website at www.hoddereducation.co.uk

First published in the Hodder Reading Project series in 2006 by Hodder Murray, an imprint of Hodder Education, a member of the Hodder Headline Group, an Hachette Livre UK Company, 338 Euston Road, London NW1 3BH.

Impression number   10 9 8 7 6 5
Year   2011 2010 2009 2008 2007

Cover photo: Haunted House © Simon Marsden/Simon Marsden Archive.
Internal artwork © Gary Andrews.
Typeset by Transet Ltd, Coventry, England.
Printed in Great Britain by CPI, Bath.

A catalogue record for this title is available from the British Library

ISBN-13: 978 0 340 91578 3

Contents

1

An Old Package

It was dirty and dusty and very old.

'What is it, Dad?' said Matt.

'I don't know,
but I thought you could use it
for your History homework.'

'Let's have a look,' said Jo.
She was round at Matt's
so they could work on their History together.
They did most things together,
but so far they had done five minutes of History,
and fifty minutes of computer games.

She took it from Matt's dad,
and turned it over in her hand.
It looked like a little packet made of leather.
It was all cracked and stiff
with two straps holding it together.

'Where did you get it, Mr Smith?' asked Jo.

'The Old Manor.'

'The Old Manor?' said Matt.
'But the whole place is closed off.
You can't get in there.'

'I know you can't get in there,
and there's a reason you can't get in there!
It's a death trap!
It could fall down any second.
Nobody has lived there for years.
That's why it says "Keep Out",
and you make sure you do!'

Matt and Jo looked at each other,
but didn't say anything.
The Old Manor was just down the road from them,
and they had tried to get into it lots of times.
There were thick hedges and fences
all the way round it and big signs saying:
'Danger! Keep Out!'
That was why, of course,
they had tried to get in,
but always the sharp thorns and the barbed wire
had stopped them.

'What were you doing there, Mr Smith?'
asked Jo.

'I was checking it over.
It's got to come down next week,
to make way for new flats.
But it's a ruin,
and so we need to do it very carefully.'

That's what Matt's father did.
He worked for the Council.
He was a surveyor.
He checked buildings for cracks and rot,
and things like that.

'Well, while I was there,
a bit of the chimney fell down,
and this was in it.'

'It looks really interesting.
What do you think is inside it?'

'Why don't you open it?
But I bet it's nothing important.
These things never are.'

Just then Matt's mum called up the stairs,
and his dad went down to see what she wanted.

'Come on then,' said Matt.
'Let's open it.'

'What do you think I'm trying to do?'
Jo was tugging at the straps.

4

'Let's have a go.'
Matt took the packet,
but the leather was stiff, and the knots were tight.
'We'll have to cut them.'

They tried scissors, but that was no good,
and Matt's penknife, no good either.

'I know,' he said, and ran downstairs.
A moment later,
he was back with his dad's Stanley knife.
'Let's use this.'

It was still hard work,
sawing away at the straps.
At last the straps gave way.

'Come on then, let's open it,' said Jo.

'We've got to be careful.
We don't want to break it.'

Matt was right. It was very fragile.
Very slowly they unfolded it,
and they could see what it was.

2

A Strange Message

It was a letter, or a message.
The writing was old and faded
and in a funny style.
But one name was clear:

The Red Fox

'The Red Fox?' said Jo.
'What's that?'

'I don't know. Is it a pub?
What else is there?' said Matt.

7

They studied it carefully,
but the writing was really old-fashioned.
Bits of it were faded so much,
they couldn't read it at all.

'That's a *p* isn't it?
And that's an *f*, a capital *F*,' said Matt.

'Let's write it down,
and see if we can work it out,' said Jo.
Matt tore out the last page of his History book,
and grabbed a pencil.

'That's an *x* and that's a *t* –
it must be *Foxton* –
but I can't read the rest,' said Matt.
Foxton was the town where they lived.

They worked away at the top line,
and at last Matt sat back and said,
'Well, that's what we've got.'

```
T-  t-e  pe-pl-  -f  Foxton
```

'"Tee-tee pepple" – what's that?' said Matt.

'It's not "pepple", it's *people*,' said Jo.
'That's what it is: *To the people of Foxton.*'

'Oh right! Well, that's us.
We're the people of Foxton.
What's the next bit?' said Matt.

```
My  tr--s-re
```

'What's that? "My tresser"?
My "tressle"? *My treas …*'
Matt saw what it was before he had even finished.
'*My treasure*. Oh wow! It's about treasure.'

This was exciting now,
and the writing suddenly seemed
a lot easier to read.
In five minutes they had copied
all the bits they could read:

My tr—s-re will keep yo-
all y—r lif-.
If yo- w-nt it,
y-u must fol-ow The Red Fox
in t-e Old Man—.

'Well, I still don't understand it,' said Matt.
'My treasure will keep "yo"?
What does that mean?'

'Keep **you**. *My treasure will keep* **you**,*'*
Jo explained.

'But who? Whose treasure?' said Matt.

'I don't know. It doesn't say,' said Jo,
'but it *will keep you* … er … *all your life.*
That's it:
My treasure will keep you all your life.
All your life!
It must be worth thousands … millions!
What's next?
If you want it,
you must follow The Red Fox in the Old Man.
So if you follow this Red Fox in the Old Man,
you get the treasure.
And it'll keep you all your life!' said Jo.

'But it still doesn't make sense,' said Matt,
'In the first place, who is this old man?
And in the second place,
how can you follow a fox into an old man?'

'The Old Manor!' said Jo.

'That's what it means.

Look there,

where the letters have got smudged.

It must mean the Old Manor.

You've got to follow *The Red Fox in the Old Manor*.'

'But what Red Fox?'

Jo said nothing.

She had been getting excited,

thinking of a huge treasure.

But Matt was right.

Who? What treasure?

What Red Fox?

'I know,' she said, 'let's try the internet.'

3

The Red Fox!

'Try *Foxton* first,' said Matt.
'There might be something about a Red Fox in that.'

'OK,' said Jo.
She typed it in, and pressed *Search*.
'Here we are – *Foxton: The History*.
Perfect! Let's try that.'
She clicked the mouse,
and read from the screen,
'Foxton is a small town in the Midlands.
It took its name from the Fox family,
who lived in the Old Manor.
It has a market, a …'

'Boring, boring!' said Matt.

'We don't have to read it.

We just want to find something about a Red Fox.'

Jo scrolled down the screen.

She seemed to be doing it for ages.

She was just going to say there was nothing there when *The Red Fox* appeared in blue print.

'Look, there it is,' said Jo.

'What does it say?' asked Matt.

Jo clicked on the words, and read:

Sir John Fox (17th century).
Landowner, thief and murderer,
the most hated man in Foxton …

'That's more like it,' said Matt.

'"Thief and murderer" – I like that!'

Jo read on:

He owned Foxton and all the land
around it. He was called the Red Fox
because of the cruel way he treated
his tenants. He kept the food they
had grown, and sold it for himself.
Many starved to death. But as he
grew older he became sorry for what
he had done. He promised to give a
great treasure to the people of
Foxton, but they killed him before he
could do so. Driven wild by their
hunger, the people turned on him,
and killed him in his own house. The
treasure, if ever there was a treasure,
was never found.

They said nothing for a moment.
It was hard to take it all in.

Then Matt said,
'If this is right, then this,'
picking up the package,
'is from this Sir John Fox, the Red Fox.
It's his last letter.
It says the treasure is in the Old Manor.'

He turned to Jo.
His face was glowing.
'And we're going there to find it!'

4

Inside the Lair

Jo stood on her toes.
She could just see some crumbling chimneys
over the hedge.
But that was all.
They had walked around it twice now,
but they couldn't find any way through.

Jo wasn't sure about being there at all,
after what Matt's dad had said.
She thought they ought to have told their parents,
or a teacher, but Matt had said,
'We're only going to have a look.
We're not going to do anything stupid.
And we don't want anyone else to find the treasure.'

'How did your dad get in?' asked Jo.

'He had a key,' said Matt.
There was a gate in the fence.
It was bolted with a big, old padlock.
Matt shook it,
and then jumped back in surprise.
It had come open in his hand.

'How did that happen?' said Matt.
'I've tried it lots of times before.'
They looked at the lock.
It was old and rusty.
Matt's dad must have closed it,
but it hadn't locked.
They looked up and down the road.
It was empty.
They slipped open the bolt,
slid through the gate and closed it behind them.
They were in!

'We've still got to get through the hedge,' said Jo.

'Well, my dad must have done it somehow.'

There was a sort of path.
But it was overgrown and difficult to follow.
It was very dark,
and there were sharp thorns on either side.
In a few minutes they were lost.
They didn't know which way was back, or forward,
and their arms and legs
were all scratched and torn.
And then suddenly they stumbled
out of the darkness into the light.

In front of them was the Old Manor.

There was hardly any roof.
And not a lot of wall either,
just lots of rubble with bushes growing out of it.
The windows were long gone.
This was all that was left
of the home of the Red Fox.
But even so,
Jo could feel a sense of him about the place.
This was where he was killed.

In front of them was a great stone arch,
and through it the ruin beyond,
open to the sky.
Above the arch was something
that made Matt grip Jo's arm and point.
A face!
The face of a fox carved into the stone!
Or maybe a man,
because although the stone was old and worn,
they could still see the evil in the narrow, cruel eyes.

Jo felt as though a cold hand had touched her.
She was very afraid.
But then she gritted her teeth.
They were only looking, after all,
and she took Matt's hand firmly.
'Come on,' she said,
and they passed through the arch
into the Old Manor itself.

Matt's dad was right.
It was very dangerous.
In many places the floor had gone,
in others only a tottering wall was left.
It was much bigger than they thought.
Room after room,
some with floors, some without,
some with rotting old doors still in place,
most with nothing.
As they looked, there was a sudden rumble,
and a wall somewhere at the back
crashed to the ground.

They knew they shouldn't be there,
treasure or no treasure,
yet something drew them on.
Jo could feel it even more,
as if after all this time
the Red Fox was still there,
watching them in his lair.

And the Red Fox was there,
all around them,
because on the walls, above the doors,
even on the floor,
were carvings of a fox.
Sometimes the body, sometimes just the face.
Sometimes looking at them,
sometimes turned away.
But always there.

'You can't get away from him,' whispered Matt.
'The people must have felt
he was looking at them all the time.'

'That's how he controlled them,' said Jo.

'Not forever, though.
They killed him in the end.'

'Perhaps they were trying to get the treasure.'

The treasure.
That was why they were there.
To find it. But how?

'What shall we do now?' said Matt.

'Let's have another look at the message,'
said Jo.

Matt brought out the sheet,
and opened it out:

> My treasure will keep you
> all your life.
> If you want it,
> you must follow The Red Fox
> in the Old Manor.

'My treasure will keep you all your life,'
Matt read out.
'If you want it,
you must follow The Red Fox in the Old Manor.
Well, that's what we're doing.
We want it, and we've come into the Old Manor.
So what do we do now?
It could be anywhere.'

All they could see were the carvings of the Red Fox.

'This is hopeless,' said Matt.
'This place is a wreck.
Even if there was any treasure,
it would be buried under all these ruins.'

Jo looked around.
The foxes were grinning at her now,
laughing even.
Some of them were looking at her,
and some of them were turned away,
or looking back over their shoulder
almost as if they wanted her to follow them.

'Of course,' she said suddenly.
'We're stupid!'

'Who's stupid?'

'We are! Don't you see?
We've got to follow the Red Fox.
That's what it says – *follow The Red Fox*,
so that's what we do.'

'But how?' asked Matt.

'Look!' said Jo.

On either side of the fireplace
there was a doorway.
Over the left hand one
was a fox face staring straight back at them,
but over the other
the fox was looking over its shoulder at them
as if it was walking into the next room.

'See!' said Jo.
'It's that way. It wants us to follow it.'

'You're right,' said Matt.
They went through the doorway on the right.

In the next room
there were three doorways,
but two of them were ruins
and if there had been anything carved above them,
there was nothing now.
But above the third
was a fox looking towards the right.

'Let's go that way,' said Matt,
and they went through the doorway,
and turned right.
They were in an old passage
with several doorways leading off it.
None of them had any foxes above them,
but carved in the floor in one of the doorways,
and now very worn,
was a fox walking through it.

'It works,' said Matt.
'You're right.
The foxes are leading us through the Old Manor.'

And so they carried on.
But it wasn't easy.
Sometimes there were whole floors
that had fallen in,
and they had to creep their way round the walls.
Sometimes the rooms were so ruined
there were no carvings left at all,
and they had to guess.
But even though they went
in and out of rooms without any clues,
they would always find another fox in the end,
and pick up the trail again.

In the excitement they forgot the danger.
They forgot they were going
deeper and deeper into the lair of the Red Fox.

5

A Dead-End

They seemed to have followed hundreds of foxes
when they came to a little room
with nothing in it at all.
There were no ways out,
and no carvings on the walls.
It was a dead-end.
They went round and round the walls,
and back the way they had come,
but there was nothing.

Jo sunk down on the floor.
'I'm sure we were going the right way.'

Matt sat down next to her.
'Perhaps we missed something.'

'We didn't, I'm sure.
There wasn't anything,' said Jo.

'Well, what do we do now?' asked Matt.

'I don't know.'
She couldn't face going back and trying again.

She tapped on a very uneven stone
in the middle of the floor.
'Where are you, Mr Red Fox?
Where's the treasure?'
She tapped harder.
'Go on! Tell us!'

'Jo, that's hollow!' said Matt.

'What?'

'Listen.'
Matt tapped on another stone.
There was a dead thud.
Then he tapped on the middle one,
and the sound changed to a sort of ringing.

'See? And look –
it's so worn you can hardly see it,
but isn't that a fox's face in the middle?'

They stepped back to look.
'You're right,' said Jo.

They scratched around the stone
with Matt's penknife.
It wasn't cemented in –
there was only dirt and moss around it.
They dug away,
and found that on the edge
below the fox's head was a little space,
into which Matt could just fit his hand.

'Do you think this is it?
I'm going to have a try.'
Matt gripped the stone, and heaved.
Nothing. He tried again.
Again nothing.

'Let me have a go,' said Jo.
She put all her strength into it,
but the stone wouldn't budge.

'Hang on,' said Matt.

'I can get my hand into there as well.'

Matt reached down,

and found space for his hand next to Jo's.

'Let's do it together.

After three. One … two … three!'

Nothing.

'Again! One … two … three!'

The stone suddenly gave way,

and so easily that they both lost their balance

and were thrown on to the floor.

But the stone was open like a great trap-door.

They crept to the edge and peered over,
and fell back choking.
Out of the hole came the stench of long-dead air,
trapped there for centuries.

When it had cleared a little,
they looked again.
It was dark and gloomy.
They could not see the bottom,
but stretching down into the darkness
was a narrow, spiral staircase.

'I've got a torch,' said Matt.

'Are you going down?'
asked Jo nervously.

'I will if you will,' said Matt.

'All right, but it's a bit scary,' said Jo.

Matt's torch was only small.
They flashed it around,
but couldn't see anything through the darkness.

'Come on, then,' said Matt,
and carefully stepped through the opening.
Step by step he sunk out of Jo's sight.
Very nervously she followed,
clinging onto the stone as she went down.

In fact it was only a few steps.
'I've reached the bottom,' said Matt,
and shone the torch to help Jo.
In a moment or two she was standing next to him
at the bottom of the stairs.
Above them
there was some light from the opening.
But all around was darkness.

6

Terror!

Matt shone his torch around.
They were standing at one end of a long room.
They couldn't see the other end.
Along the walls,
stacked two or three deep,
were huge stone jars.

'This is it,' said Matt,
'the Red Fox's treasure!'

They crept over to the first of the jars.
It was massive, nearly as tall as they were.

'Do you think they're full of gold?' asked Matt.

'I don't know,' said Jo.

'Are you going to see?' Matt asked.

'I don't like to.'
And she didn't.
All the time she had been in the Old Manor,
she'd had a feeling that somehow
the Red Fox was there, with them.
She knew it was silly,
he had been dead for hundreds of years,
but even so …

And now she felt it even more.
It wasn't just the dark, it was something else.
This was the place of the Red Fox's treasure,
the centre of his world.
This was where he had been killed.
He had been the last person here.
The last feet to have come down those stairs,
the last hands to have opened that trapdoor,
were his.
Or perhaps he was still here?
Jo gulped.
Perhaps he hadn't been killed,
but was still down here?
Or his body? A skeleton?

'Go on, have a look,' said Matt.
Jo tried to get a grip on herself,
but more and more she seemed to sense him,
the Red Fox.

She reached forward,
and put her hand in.
Was it gold? Or silver?
No, something dry and dusty.
Then she heard it, and froze.

A footstep!

Matt had heard it too.
'What's that?'

They clung together,
hardly daring to breathe.
Footsteps, very quiet at first,
but very distinct –
one after another,
very slow and very careful.
And coming out of the darkness
straight towards them.

The footsteps came on, and on,
until suddenly they were above them,
and passed over.
A head appeared in the square of light
at the top of the stairs.

'Matt! Jo! Are you down there?'

7

The Secret of the Treasure

Matt's dad was angry and relieved
at the same time.
He was hugging both of them.
'We didn't know where you were.
Your mum was in a panic, Jo.
We thought you two were with her,
and she thought you were with us.
Don't ever do anything like that again.'

They were standing outside the Old Manor.
The sun was bright to their eyes
after the gloom inside.

'Do you know how dangerous that was?
I thought I told you.
What were you thinking of?'

He had made them come out straight away,
and wouldn't listen until they were outside.

'But Dad, we found the treasure,' said Matt.

'What treasure?
What are you talking about?'

And so they told Matt's dad the whole story,
from the leather packet
to getting through the gate,
from following the Red Fox carvings on the walls,
to discovering the treasure itself.

'And what is it, this treasure of yours?'

Jo still had her hand clenched.
She held it up, and opened it.
They all peered.

'Why, it's just dirt,' said Matt.

'No, it isn't,'
said his dad after looking more carefully.

'They're seeds,' his dad continued.
'A bit dried up, but that's what they are.
Look, that's wheat, and barley,
and there's corn.'

'But that's not treasure,' said Matt.

And then Jo understood.

'But it is! It is!
This is the treasure of the Red Fox.
Don't you see?
My treasure will keep you all your life!
The Red Fox really was sorry.
All his life he had made the people suffer,
made them starve.
At the end
he wanted to give them something back.
Not gold or silver,
but something much more precious,
something that *will keep you all your life* – food!
Food they could eat,
and food they could plant,
so they would never be hungry again.
That's the real treasure of the Red Fox!'